DETAINED

DETAINED

CLAIRE AINSLIE

DARBY CREEK
MINNEAPOLIS

Darby Creek
A division of Lerner Publishing Group, Inc.
241 First Avenue North
Minneapolis, MN 55401 USA

For reading levels and more information, look up this title at www.lernerbooks.com.

Image credits: kutaytanir/Getty Images; lazy clouds/Shutterstock.com; art of line/Shutterstock.com; Alexander Lysenko/Shutterstock.com; andvasiliev/Shutterstock.com; Siarhei Tolak/Shutterstock.com; STILLFX/Shutterstock.com; primiaou/Shutterstock.com; lineartestpilot/Shutterstock.com; palform/Shutterstock.com; Tiwat K/Shutterstock.com.

Main body text set in Janson Lt Std 12/17.5.
Typeface provided by Adobe Systems.

Library of Congress Cataloging-in-Publication Data
Names: Ainslie, Claire, 1992– author.
Title: Detained / Claire Ainslie.
Description: Minneapolis : Darby Creek, [2019] | Series: AI High | Summary: Angry over being treated badly by humans, android Max is caught vandalizing AI High and sent to detention, where human Oliver stands up for him, forcing Max to rethink his views.
Identifiers: LCCN 2018047439 (print) | LCCN 2018052357 (ebook) | ISBN 9781541556966 (eb pdf) | ISBN 9781541556928 (lb : alk. paper) | ISBN 9781541572911 (pb : alk. paper)
Subjects: | CYAC: Robots—Fiction. | Prejudices—Fiction. | Conduct of life—Fiction. | High schools—Fiction. | Schools—Fiction.
Classification: LCC PZ7.1.A365 (ebook) | LCC PZ7.1.A365 Det 2020 (print) | DDC [Fic]—dc23

LC record available at https://lccn.loc.gov/2018047439

Manufactured in the United States of America
1-46126-43501-1/18/2019

TO MY SISTER, WHO ISN'T AN ANDROID,
BUT MIGHT BE AN ALIEN

SIX MONTHS AGO, THE US GOVERNMENT OFFICIALLY RECOGNIZED A GROUP OF ANDROIDS WITH ARTIFICIAL INTELLIGENCE AS A RACE OF LIVING BEINGS. These androids look exactly like humans—except for their glowing purple eyes. They have even been built to age like real humans. The first generation of adult androids have combined their programming to produce a second generation of androids: teenagers, kids, and even babies. They aren't entirely machine or entirely human but somewhere in between.

Originally, androids lived in shacks on the outskirts of towns. Recently, the government offered them housing in sectioned-off neighborhoods. Humans are upset about being displaced from their homes, and androids are frustrated that human police officers are patrolling their new neighborhoods. Protests have turned violent. Riots have broken out in the streets.

In an effort to help androids and humans coexist, the government has launched a pilot program for android students in several high schools across the country. One of those high schools is Fitzgerald High School, nicknamed AI High.

Now, about eight hundred teen androids—almost one-fifth of the school population—attend Fitzgerald High. Android students take classes to learn about living in human society. Humans and androids also take classes together in hopes of building understanding and harmony. But many from both sides are reluctant about this new program.

With the teenage androids participating in a school system for the first time in their lives and the tension between the groups simmering, every day brings uncertainty.

"Shhh!" I hissed at Lily as she smothered a giggle with her hands. The single hallway light still on in the science wing of AI High glinted off her purple eyes as she threw a mischievous look over her shoulder at me. I looked around nervously, convinced a teacher would suddenly appear. We were not supposed to be in the school this late at night.

Excitement fizzed through my veins, and I felt like everything was moving in slow motion. I hoisted the garbage bag full of toilet paper rolls over my shoulder.

"Max, relax, there's no one here!" whispered Lily, but she still looked down the hallway toward where the lockers disappeared into the dark.

I watched my best friend pull a couple of hairpins out of her bun and bend over the doorknob. I could just barely read the plaque on the door that said "Chemistry." A wrinkled paper sign taped above it added "Human." I rolled my eyes. As if any of us androids would ever need to take Chemistry. Math and science were programmed into us. It was just another reminder of how the humans actually felt about us.

I missed my old school—there weren't any humans there. No one yelling insults at me in the hall or calling me "droid" instead of Max or doing the robot when they saw me coming. When my parents told me I had to come to AI High, I didn't talk to them for a week. I don't care if integration is a "step forward for society" like they're always telling me. I just don't want to be seen as a freak anymore.

Lily let out a squeak of satisfaction as the lock clicked open and the doorknob turned then quickly stifled the sound. A street light shone through the window, illuminating rows of lab desks with Bunsen burners arranged neatly on top. Shelves of shining glass beakers and test tubes lined the back wall.

I closed the door quietly behind me and let out a breath I didn't know I'd been holding, feeling some of the tension go out of my shoulders. I'd always followed the rules until this. There had never been anything I wanted to do that was worth getting in trouble for. The last couple of months at AI High had changed that, so when Lily had suggested TP-ing a human classroom, I'd bought the toilet paper before we'd even picked a date.

I dropped my bag of toilet paper on the ground in front of me and grinned. "Ready?" I asked Lily.

She just grinned back and dug a couple rolls of toilet paper out of the bag.

The first throw was glorious. I watched the paper sail through the air in a huge arc, draping itself over a bookshelf and several desks. Lily went straight for the teacher's desk, wrapping its legs in toilet paper with a wicked look on her face before making sure she covered the whole top just as thoroughly.

We used every single roll I'd brought. The tile floor disappeared under a carpet of white squares and paper hung from every bit of furniture like a huge spider web. I knew this wasn't necessarily right, but it felt good. It was like I'd thrown away some of the insults with every roll of toilet paper. As much as I loved sitting at home playing my guitar, this was a different kind of fun.

"Why haven't I ever done this before?" I asked Lily, buzzing with the thrill of our adventure.

"Ummm, because you're Mr. Perfect?" she said, pretending to think really hard.

I laughed, for once not worrying what my parents would say or what would happen if we got caught. Right at that moment it seemed pretty worth it, no matter what happened.

"I just want to give the humans a taste of their own medicine. They think they're so much better than we are, but I guarantee we could run things better than they do." I ignored the little voice in my head telling me that vandalizing one of their classrooms might not make the androids seem like we'd be better leaders. Besides, toilet paper was a lot less destructive than some of the things humans had done to androids over the years.

"I'm sure we could," said Lily. "Androids don't have all that human baggage from centuries of war. We'd be able to make decisions with a way more level head. I'll settle for this for now, though. We've got to get their attention somehow."

I laughed with her, trying to imagine a world where the humans actually treated us like equals and didn't just talk about it.

Lily was standing in the back of the room. She pulled out her phone. "Get over here, Max! I don't think you want to be in my photographic evidence."

I hurried around the lab desks, muffling an exclamation as I banged my hip into the corner of one. Lily just rolled her eyes at me. She was used to my clumsiness by now. My parents tried to find the flaw in my coding, but after one attempt accidentally disabled my ability to walk forward, they decided to stop tinkering. I'd had to walk around backward for three days while they recovered my original code.

She snapped a couple of pictures on her phone, smirking a little. "They aren't going to know what hit them," she said. "We should have—"

"Wait," I hissed, holding up a hand to stop her. "Did you hear something?"

She paused for a second listening, but neither of us heard anything. "You're paranoid," she said. "There's no one—"

She stopped when we both heard the hum—one of those big floor buffing machines the janitors use to clean the hallways. We froze, staring at each other. I was sure my eyes were twice their usual size. *My* programming told me to run, but I couldn't seem to move.

"Come on!" she said, her eyes flashing. "We've got to get out of here!"

Her voice sounded far away in my panic, but I think I nodded. I watched her run to the door and look carefully out the window.

After a few seconds she ducked, motioning for me to do the same. I followed her lead, flinching as the window darkened as the janitor passed.

The sound of the machine faded. Lily got up and came back to me, grabbing my hand to pull me to my feet.

"Let's go," she whispered. "He should be around the corner by now. We can make a run for it."

This sounded sensible, but I couldn't shake the feeling that leaving this room would mean getting caught. Logically, I knew that staying here too long would inevitably mean getting caught too, but my fear paralyzed me.

"Seriously, Max, snap out of it! We've got to go!" She sounded a little annoyed now. That was fair. I was annoyed with myself. She tugged hard on my hand, but it slipped out of her grasp and she tripped. I watched in horror as her momentum carried her into one of the shelves of beakers.

The crash shattered not only the glass but the silence in the room as well. Then, a new silence fell in the hallway—the floor buffer had been turned off. Lily met my gaze. "Go!" I said. "I'll follow you!"

The glass had cut off the path directly to her, so I had to find my way through the maze of desks and toilet paper. I heard the door open as Lily reached it and watched her round the corner. I could hear a second set of footsteps in the hall, coming closer to the chemistry lab. I should have kept my eyes on where I was going. I slipped on the toilet paper and fell, crashing into a desk. My ribs throbbed with the impact and I wheezed, unable to take a full breath. The corner of the desk had knocked all the wind out of me.

I was still struggling to my feet when the light from the hall was blocked, darkening the room. I avoided looking at the janitor standing in the doorway.

"I'm still here, even if you're not looking at me," said the janitor in a deep voice.

Lily spends her whole life breaking rules and getting away with it, and then the first time I try anything, I get caught. Just my luck.

Slowly, I raised my own purple eyes to the janitor's brown ones.

"A droid. I knew it," growled the janitor. "I hope you know I won't be the one cleaning this up. It's bad enough I have to clean up the normal messes you lot make. If I didn't need this job . . ."

I could feel my anger starting to choke me. Humans like him were the worst. The ones who hadn't realized that society was moving on. The ones who couldn't let go of being "better" than us. He looked at me like I was a cockroach. This was why I hadn't wanted to come here. No matter what they'd said about a "supportive environment" and "a new beginning," I'd known it wouldn't be like that. There were always going to be some people who hated us for being different.

I shoved the anger away, clenching my fists. Yelling at the janitor would only make things worse.

"First thing tomorrow I'm reporting you to the principal," said the janitor. "And then I'll make you clean up your mess." He smiled, but it wasn't a kind smile. It only made him look meaner. "Your name, now."

For a moment I thought about refusing to tell him. If he didn't know who I was, how would he find out? Then I remembered that the school had all our pictures on file, and if he really wanted to, he'd be able to identify me. And it wasn't like I was going to be able to shove past him and make a run for it anyway.

"Max Anderson," I said, avoiding his eyes.

The janitor pulled out his phone and made a note, nodding to himself with a satisfied smirk. He jerked his head at me. "Now get out."

I didn't wait for him to say it again. I brushed past him, toilet paper still trailing from my shoe, and hurried down the hallway without looking back. Away from his nasty glare, some of my satisfaction came back. So what if I had to do detention from now until the end of the year? The humans deserved everything I could throw at them, and I was just getting started.

The janitor did exactly what he said he would. Ten minutes into first period the next day, the phone rang in our classroom. Mrs. Johnson answered and frowned, looking at me. "The principal needs to see you in her office," she said.

I ignored the whispers from my classmates and grabbed my backpack. The weight of it on my shoulder was nothing compared to the weight of my feet trying to move me to the door.

There were two empty chairs in front of the principal's desk. Ms. Roberts, the principal, was human, and her brown eyes were usually cheerful. Right now she looked like her cat had died.

"Sit down, please, Max," she said.

I sat carefully, like the chair might try to bite me. She looked at me, waiting for me to make eye contact with her before she said anything else.

When I finally did, she said, "I'm disappointed in you. When I took this job, I was so excited to help young androids and young humans connect. You have so much to offer each other."

A wave of anger washed over me. I knew I should keep my mouth shut and take her lecture and punishment, but I started to speak before I could help myself.

"You talk about wanting us all to get to know each other and be a big happy family, but you don't even notice what your precious human students are doing to us androids. If you refuse to see what's happening, you're not actually doing anything to help us." I snapped my mouth shut. Her eyes had narrowed, but her voice was cotton-candy sweet when she spoke.

"I'm sorry you feel that way, but this school prides itself on being a safe place for both humans and androids. Maybe you can think of more constructive ways to channel your feelings during detention, which is where you'll be every day after school for the next two weeks. If you do anything like this again, you can expect detention for the rest of the month."

I swallowed the sour taste in my mouth and just nodded. Typical human. If she wouldn't listen to what I said, I'd find other ways to get my point across. Detention wouldn't stop me.

* * *

There were other people in the classroom when I got to detention after school. The only android in the room sat apart from the humans. They had their backs to her, but she didn't look interested in talking to them anyway. The humans—three of them—stared at me when I walked in. I ignored them and went to sit by the android girl. I'd seen her around before, but I'd never talked to her.

"I'm Nora," she said, snapping a piece of gum between her teeth.

"Max," I said. I didn't really want to talk to

anyone here. I just wanted to do my time and get out.

Luckily I didn't have to say anything else because the teacher arrived. She was human, and fairly young. I think she taught math for the humans, but I'd never had a class with her.

"Good afternoon!" she said cheerfully. I stopped myself from rolling my eyes. Why was she so cheerful about supervising detention? "Now, you all know why you're here. Hopefully we'll all get along and you'll all be back to enjoying your afternoons in no time! Today we're headed to the chemistry lab. Someone vandalized it last night, and it needs to be cleaned up. You can leave your stuff here."

I could have sworn her eyes flicked over to me for a second, but they were gone so fast I wasn't sure. I let out a breath when she moved on without telling them who'd done it. The last thing I wanted was for everyone to turn on me.

"Before we head down there, I'm going to take attendance! Nora . . . Emily . . . Jackson . . . Oliver . . . and Max."

She checked off each name as we raised our hand and then hurried us out of the classroom.

We followed the teacher down the hall to the chemistry lab. In the daylight, our toilet paper masterpiece had lost some of its magic. Now it just looked like a mess. The human girl, Emily, looked horrified.

"Why do we have to clean this up?" she asked angrily. "I didn't have anything to do with it! I'm only here because I was late for class!"

"We decided it was better for you to do something constructive with your time," said the teacher calmly. "I'm sure it won't kill you. Garbage bags are on the desk, there." She pointed. "I'll be right next door grading if anyone needs anything. And I'll be checking on you."

I was glad they didn't know the mess was mine—the look Emily was giving the teacher's back was deadly. I did my best to look angry too. I didn't want to draw any attention to myself.

The quiet boy, Oliver, was already stuffing wads of toilet paper into a garbage bag.

I grabbed a bag of my own and started cleaning up without saying anything else.

"Here, Emily," said Jackson, passing her a bag. She took it, scowling, but didn't open it. "Come on," he added. "The sooner we finish, the sooner we can go home."

She wrinkled her nose is disgust. "Why aren't you more upset about this?" she asked Jackson. "So you don't do your homework. Why should you be cleaning up after whoever did this?"

He shrugged and smiled slightly. "You should chill. It's not that bad. I'd rather do this than have to sit at a desk without talking for an hour."

Emily shoved some toilet paper roughly into her bag. The end was still hanging out. "I bet it was one of those droids," she said, glaring at Nora and me. "Who else would do this?"

"You're probably right," said Jackson. "They think they don't have to follow the rules. My dad says they think they're better than we are because things like math are programmed into them so they never have to learn them. He says it makes them lazy. They never have to work for anything."

I looked down at the ground, trying to ignore them. Nora was tense next to me, and I could practically hear the air crackling around her. I wanted to scream at them so badly I felt sick. *Yes, a droid did it! Because you act like that! Why would we respect someone who thinks we're so awful?*

"Maybe it was a human," said Nora, loud enough that everyone could hear her. "They're the ones who screw everything up for everyone else. That's what they've done forever."

"At least we've been around basically forever," said Emily, laughing nastily.

"It's too bad we won't be around to see who lasts longer," I said, too angry to keep my mouth shut any longer. "But I'm willing to bet it won't be humans." We all glared at each other.

"I can't believe I'm the one in here for mouthing off," said Nora under her breath. "She's way worse than I am."

The sound of Oliver shaking open a new trash bag broke the tension. "If you don't mind, I'd like some help so we can all get out of here," he said, and then went back to cleaning up without another word.

We were all working in uncomfortable silence when the teacher poked her head around the door frame. "How's it going?" she said cheerfully. "I thought you'd be a little farther by now." A little frown wrinkled her forehead. "Make sure you tie the trash bags up when they're full. You can set them in the hallway so they're out of your way."

She disappeared again, and Nora rolled her eyes at me so hard that I couldn't even see her purple irises anymore. "I don't know why she has to act all cheery. It's annoying."

I just shrugged.

Emily and Jackson were cleaning the back of the classroom when Emily shrieked. You'd have thought she was dying from the way she went on. "Oh my god, I'm bleeding!" she wailed. "Why didn't anyone say there was broken glass back here?"

She held her hand up in the air, and she actually did have blood running down her wrist.

"Here," said Oliver. He pressed a wad of clean toilet paper to the cut and then went right back to cleaning. Emily didn't even thank him.

"Did she not notice he's human?" Nora muttered. I couldn't stop myself from letting out a snort.

"What, you think it's funny that my hand is mangled?" said Emily, outraged. "I guess that would make sense, since I'm not sure you actually have real feelings. Maybe we were right before when we said you're just extra advanced robots."

"Just ignore them," said Jackson soothingly to Emily. "They don't matter."

I couldn't speak, I was so mad. How dare she call us robots! I knew there were some people who still thought that, but they didn't usually come out and say it. Ever since the government recognized us as equal it had become a lot less acceptable to say stuff like that.

Supposedly there were some humans who were on our side. My parents said they'd known a lot of them when they were campaigning for equal rights. But I was never sure that humans weren't still thinking awful things about me, no matter what they said. Some people thought it was cool to support the android cause. How was I supposed to know if they actually believed in it? Maybe they just wanted their friends to think they were edgy or whatever.

No one spoke for the rest of the hour it took us to clean up. We all just wanted to get out of there as soon as possible.

"Excellent job!" said the teacher when she came back. "I'm so glad to see you all working together!" She smiled so wide I was sure I could see every one of her teeth. I heard Emily let out a huge sigh behind me. "Now, I hope I don't see any of you here any time soon! I know some of you are frequent flyers"—she looked at Jackson and narrowed her eyes—"try to keep yourselves out of trouble. All right, get out of here!"

I grabbed my stuff, so angry that I was surprised I hadn't blown a fuse yet. Ideas for new ways to get back at the humans were already bouncing around my head. I'd give them a taste of their own medicine.

I lay low for a week, but detention with Emily and Jackson had only made me angrier at the whole human population of AI High. Nothing huge had happened at detention since the first day, but Emily and Jackson didn't get any nicer either, and their snide comments made me angrier and angrier. I did my best to keep my mouth shut—I didn't want to make things even worse.

Lily was busy, but I decided it was time for some more action. Humans were never going to change. They were always going to treat us like we were a bit of dog poop they stepped in. Minding my own business hadn't worked, so

I decided to fight back. I only made it through a week of detention before I pulled another prank. I really didn't want to get caught this time, so I washed my hands about a hundred times afterward, but they still smelled like rotting fish. That wasn't the reason I got caught, though.

I got the idea for the fish when I went for a walk around the pond near my house. There were some dead fish washed up on shore, and the smell was so bad I had to hold my breath until I was well past them. The next day, I bought as much fish as I could carry and left them in the garage for a few days to rot.

When it finally smelled bad enough, I could put my plan into action. I would have gotten away with it, too, except that they put up more security cameras after Lily and I broke in to TP the chemistry lab. I thought I'd gotten away with it until I was called in to the principal's office first thing in the morning. Ms. Roberts showed me the footage. I had to force myself not to smile as I watched it.

At least I managed to get all my fish into humans' lockers. Since this used to be a human-only school they still had old passcode lockers for the students, so they were really easy for an android with hacking skills like me to break into.

When everyone got to school this morning, the smell was so bad that people were throwing up. That didn't help the stink. At least they couldn't leave the puke for the detention kids to clean up—that would have been too much of a health hazard. I was hoping that cleaning up the rotten fish would be too urgent to leave for the detention kids, but I was wrong.

There were rubber gloves and buckets waiting in the detention classroom when I got there. Luckily there were also a few more people than last time. They sat in a corner, talking quietly. Clearly they were all friends.

I was surprised to see Emily, Jackson, Nora, and Oliver all back as well. I didn't have any classes with any of them, but Lily told me Nora mouthed off to the human teacher in Android/Human Relations almost every day.

Emily and Jackson were probably the same with being late and never doing homework. I couldn't figure out what Oliver was in for, though.

A new teacher was supervising detention today. He looked grumpy and tired. He took attendance right away and then directed us to grab buckets and gloves. We filled the buckets with soap and hot water in a janitor's closet and then made our way to the fishy lockers.

If anything, the smell had gotten worse since this morning. I fought the urge to laugh and gag at the same time. If the teachers weren't going to say who did it, I wasn't going to give myself away.

"This has got to be some sort of abuse," said Emily through the shirt she had pulled over her nose. "This is disgusting!"

"Unless you're allergic to fish, I don't want to hear it," said the grumpy teacher. "Get moving. We'll all be happier with this stench gone."

This teacher didn't leave us alone. He pulled a desk into the hall and sat where he could see us over his stack of papers. He was far enough away, though, that he couldn't hear the whispering.

"Do you think this is the same person as the chem lab?" asked Jackson as he lazily wiped out someone's locker with the soapy water.

"It's obviously one of the droids," hissed Emily. "These are all human lockers. Someone is targeting us." She stared at me and Nora over Jackson's shoulder.

"People vandalize stuff at other schools too," Nora shot back. "Why does it have to be an android?"

"Seriously?" said Emily. "All of these pranks have been directed at humans and made our lives harder. It's pretty obvious to me who the culprit is. Droids don't care about humans. They don't appreciate everything we've given them. I would have thought that giving your kind basic rights was enough, but you're all so greedy. Jackson's right. You all want everything handed to you."

"Ouch!" I said as I scraped my knuckles against the edge of the locker's latch. I'd been scrubbing more and more violently with every word out of Emily's mouth.

I glared at her. She hadn't even gotten her rag wet yet. She wasn't even pretending to work.

"There are plenty of lazy humans, though, aren't there," I said angrily, trying to keep my voice quiet so the teacher wouldn't hear. "I don't see you doing anything."

"I'm not lazy," she said. "This isn't my mess. The droids can clean it up."

I didn't answer her. Instead I just went back to scrubbing the locker. I knew I was the one who made the mess, but she didn't. She didn't even know for sure an android did it. I just couldn't stand that she thought she was too good for the punishment the rest of us were getting. It wasn't like she was the only one being asked to clean up. Clearly I wasn't going to change her mind about androids. It wasn't even worth talking to her.

Emily and Jackson seemed to inspire the rest of the humans in detention, and soon none of them were helping anymore. Every time the teacher looked up, though, they'd pretend to be working. Only Oliver continued to help. Emily kept shooting him looks that were almost as nasty as the ones Nora and I got.

I was struggling to reach the back of the top shelf of one of the lockers when Oliver's arm reached over me. He was at least six inches taller than me, and he didn't have any trouble reaching.

"Here, let me," he said.

I let him, but mostly because I was shocked. *I thought they all hated us.* I swallowed the urge to ask why he was doing this. "Thanks," I finally said, a little too late.

Together we made our way down the row of lockers. I cleaned the bottoms while he cleaned the tops. I could practically feel Emily and Jackson burning holes on our backs. Nora caught my eye, raising one eyebrow at me. I just shrugged. If he wanted to help, I wasn't going to stop him.

Again I wondered what Oliver had done to get himself sent to detention. He didn't really seem like the type to get in trouble, but I still didn't trust him. What if it was an act?

Maybe he wanted to live alongside androids and actually get to know us, or maybe he just selfishly wanted people to think he was a good person.

Working with Oliver made the job go quicker, but it also meant that Nora didn't talk to me. She didn't give me or Oliver the kind of nasty looks that came from Emily and Jackson, but I could feel her tension. We finished cleaning the lockers in silence.

I couldn't tell anymore if the smell of fish was on me, the lockers, or the rags, but it still stank. At least the other students wouldn't be able to blame me based on the smell—we all reeked of fish.

When the teacher finally dismissed us, I headed off toward my own locker. As I turned to go, Oliver waved at me, looking downright friendly. Awkwardly, I waved back, my mouth curling into a weird almost-smile that didn't show my teeth. It was the first time a human student had smiled at me, and it only confused me more. *What's this kid's deal?* I thought as I hurried away, my heart racing.

I kept my head down for a couple weeks after the fish incident. Then, once the humans seemed to forget about it, I hid in the bathroom after school until everyone was gone and painted "MEATHEAD HIGH" across the whole back wall of the cafeteria. I'm not an artist, so the bright red paint I used ran down the wall and looked kind of threatening. I decided that I didn't care whether they caught me or not. I wasn't ashamed of what I was doing. I had something to say, and this seemed like the only way to make people listen.

They added another month of detentions this time, since it was my third time getting in trouble. I'd have been in detention for ten weeks straight by the end. It would probably take ages to scrub the paint off the cafeteria wall, anyway. Maybe we would have to repaint it.

At lunch the next day, Lily and I sat at a table under my graffiti. She smacked my arm as I sat down and I almost dropped my tray.

"Why didn't you ask for my help with the fish or the graffiti?" she asked. She was annoyed, but she kept her voice down. "I'm the one who came up with the idea to vandalize the school in the first place!"

"What can I say, you inspired me," I replied. "You don't want to be stuck in detention with us anyway."

Her forehead was still scrunched in a frown. "I'm supposed to be your best friend. I want to help!"

"Trust me, you do not want to be in detention. And it will probably get even worse if the humans find out I'm the one who's been pulling the pranks," I said.

Lily narrowed her eyes at me. "When

people do find out, there's no way I'm letting you take all the credit."

"I wouldn't dream of it!" I said, hoping she'd let it go. Truthfully, I liked doing it alone, but there was no point starting an argument with her.

"I'm serious!" she said. "You'd better let me help you."

"Fine. I promise I'll let you help me. Next time." I hoped she'd be too busy to bring it up again for a while.

"I'm holding you to that," she said, and walked off to her next class.

* * *

Later that day in detention, I was reminded why spray-painting a wall was so inconvenient. "You're all going to scrub this wall until it shines!" the gym teacher told us as we stood in line with buckets and rags.

The regulars had shown up to detention again. Nora had gotten into a screaming match with the civics teacher and was in detention the rest of the week. I heard Jackson and Emily say that they were both in for the rest of the month because they'd made no effort to change their behavior.

Oliver was still there too. He grinned at me when we made eye contact, but then he just said hello and went to pick up his cleaning supplies.

Emily and Jackson couldn't avoid cleaning this time. The gym teacher wouldn't let them get away with it. The minute she saw their phones, she took them away and shoved sponges into their hands. "Get scrubbing," was all she said.

I thought Emily would argue, but she just stared at the teacher's back for a moment before starting to wipe half-heartedly at the paint. Jackson scrubbed violently next to her, taking his anger out on the wall.

It didn't matter how hard we scrubbed, though. I silently congratulated myself—this was going to take longer to get rid of than the other things I'd done.

"Here," I said, passing a sponge to Nora.

She rolled her eyes. "I'm so over this," she

muttered, before squeezing the extra water out of her sponge and slowly starting to clean.

"Pass me a sponge?" asked Oliver from behind me.

I grabbed one and handed it to him, feeling my face both try to smile and stay expressionless at the same time. I probably looked like I was trying not to puke.

"Thanks," he said. He turned to his section of the wall and started cleaning methodically. He didn't have much success, but he didn't look too worked up about it either. From what I'd seen so far, he was a calm person. I still couldn't figure out what he'd done to get himself into detention for so long.

We were quiet for only a few minutes. "Watch it!" said Emily. I looked up, thinking this was directed at Nora or me. Emily didn't usually sound that nasty talking to other humans.

Instead, she was glaring at Oliver. He'd dripped some soapy water on her head while he was trying to get at the highest part of the graffiti. You'd think he'd dumped a whole bucket over her from how outraged she looked. She turned to Jackson and muttered something I couldn't hear. He laughed nastily, turning around to look at Oliver.

"Quiet, you two!" yelled the teacher.

Emily and Jackson snapped back to their cleaning, but they kept glancing at Oliver. He moved as far away from them as he could. We might have made it through the rest of detention without an issue if I weren't so clumsy.

I bent over to rinse my sponge in my bucket, but I didn't see Oliver behind me. He tripped over me, knocking the bucket of water over. It flooded across the floor, soaking Emily's shoes.

She froze the same time Oliver and I did. Slowly she turned to look at us. When she saw Oliver still kneeling on the floor, she rounded on him.

If she'd been a cat, she'd have had all her fur puffed up and her ears flat. "How dare you," she hissed, trying to avoid the teacher's attention. "My shoes are ruined! They're brand new too!"

"I'm sorry," started Oliver.

"I don't care if you're sorry," said Emily.

"I didn't try to spill on you! I really just want to get this done and get out of here," said Oliver, his head down.

Emily snorted. "You're such a suck-up. I can't believe you got yourself stuck in here."

Oliver was trying to ignore her now, but I could see his face turning a little red. I tried not to listen. It wasn't my problem that Emily was awful. This had nothing to do with me. I ignored the stubborn voice in my head trying to tell me to stand up for him. Instead, I let Emily's nasty comments fade into the background, focusing on the wall.

When Jackson joined in with Emily's needling, it cut through my focus. "You know, it's kind of weird how helpful you are," he said. "You know this was the droids. So I guess you care more about them than your own people." I thought he was done, but he muttered, "Traitor," as he turned back to the wall.

"Well, it's not like you two are giving me

so many reasons to like humans," Oliver shot back unexpectedly.

"You're still one of us," said Emily. "They're ruining everything, but for some reason you don't seem worried about that."

"Maybe I don't think they're ruining things," he said.

I couldn't really believe what I was hearing. I hadn't heard a human student defend an android a single time since I started at AI High. Even most of the human teachers barely tried to make us feel welcome.

Emily and Jackson were looking at Oliver in disbelief. "I'm sorry, did I hear you right?" asked Jackson. "You don't think the droids are ruining things? Have you been paying any attention at all?"

"They're invading our lives," said Emily. "The freaks don't even stay with their own kind anymore. Everything has gotten worse here! I can't believe you're fine with droids taking opportunities that belong to us. To humans!"

"They have as much right to be here as anyone. If you can't find opportunities for yourself, maybe that's a problem with you," said Oliver quietly. His voice was soft, but he stood his ground.

All of the sudden, Emily kicked over her own bucket of soapy water, which washed over Oliver's shoes. He jumped back, but his feet were already soaked. "Oops," she said with a nasty smile.

Oliver stared at her for a couple seconds, deciding his next move. But then he just shook his head and turned back to the wall. He began scrubbing at the graffiti with the same methodical rhythm as before.

After another half hour, the teacher came over, frowning at the wall. We might as well have spent the last hour sitting at our desks for all of the progress we'd made.

"Well, I can't say I'm impressed with what you have accomplished," said the teacher. "I'll let the principle know this will have to be repainted. You all can go."

Everyone filed out of the hallway quietly. Nora nudged me with her elbow. "Can you believe Emily? It's just water, and it's not like she's got any circuits to short." She snorted. "And Jackson. He thinks we're ruining things after the mess humans have made of the whole world for, like, all of history? Can humans get any worse?" She laughed, throwing a conspiratorial look my way, but I wasn't really listening. I couldn't stop thinking about Oliver. He seemed so genuinely nice.

There was a small knot of guilt in my stomach as well. The other humans had only turned on Oliver because he'd been kind to me. Logically I knew that I wasn't responsible for Emily and Jackson's actions, but I still felt guilty. I scowled at myself. Why did I even care? If Oliver wanted to get himself exiled from the humans, that was his problem. I wasn't going to worry about it.

5

Over the next few days I poured all my energy into coming up with a new idea—old school pranks were great, but I wanted to do something different. In the end, breaking into the lockers inspired my next idea. I was a really good hacker—even for an android. Hacking into AI High's internal network was a piece of cake.

The morning after I hacked the network, I got to school early. I couldn't wait to see people's reactions. I could hardly sit still waiting for the bell to ring for first period. After Mrs. Johnson took attendance, she tried to pull up a presentation on her smart screen.

Instead of whatever she was planning to

teach, footage of a street full of androids came up. I had programmed all the smart screens to play video from one of the first android protests, back when my parents' generation was trying to get the government to recognize us as equal to humans.

"What is going on?" spluttered Mrs. Johnson. I held back a delighted laugh. The other students in the class, androids and humans, were whispering to each other.

Mrs. Johnson pushed all the buttons on her remote and all the keys on her keyboard trying to get her lecture notes to come up, but I made sure people would have to watch. The androids on the screen chanted loudly, and lines of human police officers in riot gear forced them into blocked off areas of the streets. When the protest started to turn violent, she'd had enough.

"That's it, I'll just shut it down," she said, pressing the power button.

I'd already thought of that. Instead of the screen going black, the volume just got louder. I could hear the sound of the protest video playing from other classrooms too. I tried not laugh.

"Jess!" shouted Mrs. Johnson to one of the girls by the door. "Please go get the principal." Mrs. Johnson looked around frantically, searching for the power cord, but the screens were wired directly into the wall and the cords were all behind the mounted screens, so there was no plug she could pull.

Suddenly, the lights went out and we were left with just the light coming in the windows. They'd cut the power to the building.

"When was that?" asked one of the human students I didn't know. "That has to have been ages ago, right?"

Mrs. Johnson sighed, looking like she didn't want to talk about android rights issues this early in the morning. "No, Sam, that wasn't actually that long ago. Those protests were about twenty-five years ago."

The rest of the lesson turned into a lecture on the android rights movement, which was exactly what I wanted. Mrs. Johnson definitely tried to gloss over some of the worst aspects, but it was the most anyone had talked about this stuff since I started at AI High. The human students needed to learn about some of this history.

The best part was that they couldn't prove it was me who had pulled the prank this time. All I had to do now was finish serving my time for the graffiti.

* * *

I thought today's detention would be less eventful. Emily complained like always, but Nora and I—and Oliver—did our best to stay out of her way. We were making good progress on painting the wall when everything went wrong.

People sometimes walked through the cafeteria after school while we did our detention, but they usually ignored us. Even my friend Lily didn't usually do anything more than wave at me on her way through. Today was different, though.

This time, as she walked through, Lily called out to me, "Hey, Max! Nice work on the smart screens! Your best idea yet!" She was grinning when she playfully added, "You still should have let me help, though!"

I froze. All the other students were staring at me.

I was about to deny it, but Lily was already gone.

Emily looked like she was about to spit venom at me. "This has all been you?" she asked. Her voice was ice cold.

I felt like time had slowed way down but my brain was racing into overdrive. All my muscles were tense, even though I was trying to look like Lily's comments didn't mean anything to me.

"You never said why you were here," said Jackson. His voice was calm, but it wasn't a friendly calm. It was like the calm before a storm.

I opened my mouth to deny it, but nothing came out. I was furious with Lily. Yeah, I was proud of my actions, but I wasn't about to make my life more difficult on purpose. Doing detention was one thing—even doing it with people like Emily and Jackson who would never like me anyway. But doing it with a bunch of people who hated me because they had to clean up my messes? That was *not* something I wanted to deal with.

I pushed my anger at Lily to the back of my mind. I'd deal with that later.

Still, I couldn't bring myself to own up to it with Emily and Jackson. "That's my business," I said, trying to stay calm. "Who cares why I'm here?"

"We do," said Emily. "If you've been the one making these messes, I'm so done cleaning them up."

"I don't think you really get a choice in that," I said mildly. I looked pointedly at the teacher, who was busy talking to a student who had stopped by to say hello.

She shrugged. "I guess we'll see about that."

"Oh, come on," said Nora. "If he did do it, the teachers obviously already know, and they've still got us all cleaning up. You finding out isn't going to change their minds."

"Of course you side with him," said Jackson.

"You droids are welcome to clean up each other's messes, but we aren't going to."

"Maybe you're right," I said. I didn't say it very loudly because I was trying to keep my voice from shaking with anger and nerves, but they heard me anyway. "Maybe I did all of it, but it's not like you guys don't deserve it." It still wasn't an outright confession, but I knew they'd take it as one.

"I knew it!" shrieked Emily.

This finally caught the teacher's attention. "What is going on here?" she asked, marching over to us. "Why aren't you painting?"

I thought Emily would answer right away, but the gym teacher apparently scared her. She just glared at me while we all stood silently. No one wanted to say anything at all.

Finally Oliver broke the awkward silence. "Emily and Jackson think Max is responsible for all the stuff we've had to clean up," he said.

The teacher looked at us with her arms folded over her chest. "So?" she said.

"It isn't fair to make us clean up after him when we didn't make the mess!" said Jackson.

"I don't know why you're all so worried about it," said Oliver, rolling his eyes. "You're stuck in detention anyway."

Why is he defending me again? I was grateful, but I still couldn't shake the suspicious feeling that had settled in my stomach.

"He should be responsible for cleaning up his own messes," spat Jackson. "It's unnatural for humans to clean up after droids."

"That's enough of that," said the teacher, frowning at him. "Oliver is right. It's none of your business why Max is in detention if he doesn't want to tell you. And if you weren't doing this cleanup, we'd be finding other unpleasant things for you to do. How do you feel about cleaning up the dissection kits from the biology lab?"

Emily went pale and looked like she might throw up.

"That's what I thought. Now, I don't want to hear another word about this. Do your work and leave each other alone. We'll all be much happier."

We all turned back to the wall. Even Emily

picked up a paint roller and started working, though she shot murderous looks and both me and the teacher every few minutes.

"Here," said Oliver, passing me a roller.

"Thanks," I said quietly.

"Don't let them get to you," he said. "If this stuff has been you—don't worry, you don't have to tell me—I get it. I know what it's like when you can't get anyone to listen to you."

I wasn't sure what to say to him. I still didn't want to come out and admit what I'd been doing, especially with Emily and Jackson there. I settled for muttering, "Thanks," and smiling tentatively.

I had a hard time believing Oliver could actually relate to how the androids felt at AI High, but something about his response had caught me off guard. I wanted to ask him what he meant, but it didn't seem appropriate. I was not ready to get personal with a human. Not even one who seemed nice.

"What a freak," said Emily. I thought she was talking about me until she added, "Why does he even bother talking to the stupid droids?"

"Who cares?" said Jackson. "It's obvious that this experiment isn't working. The droids'll be gone next year, and Oliver can go with them if he wants to side with them so much."

"Do they ever shut up?" said Nora under her breath. "We could be out of here by now if they'd just quit complaining and help properly."

Luckily Emily and Jackson didn't hear her. Even with the teacher watching us closely, I think they might have lost it.

"Just ignore them," I said back to her. "We get to leave in ten minutes anyway."

We managed to cover the M, E, and A of MEATHEAD HIGH before the teacher finally let us go. I couldn't get out of there fast enough.

The next day I finished detention—uneventful for once—and then met Lily outside the school.

"I had an idea for a great prank!" said Lily before I'd even said hello. "We should hack—"

I stopped her before she could finish. "I'm really not in the mood today," I said.

"What do you mean, you're not in the mood? I thought you were really into it! And it doesn't seem like you minded detention much," she said, looking disappointed.

"That was before everyone in detention found out they were cleaning up my messes!" I said. It came out a bit angrier than I meant it to. "Did you think that would go over well?

Especially with the humans in there who already hated me?"

I let out a shaky breath, trying to calm down. Even though I knew Lily hadn't meant to make things worse for me, I couldn't help being mad.

"How was I supposed to know they didn't know who was doing it?" she said defensively. "You were so proud of yourself around me. I thought they must have already known. I was trying to support you!"

"I only told you! The teachers didn't even say anything. Everyone knew it wouldn't help the situation in detention since no one could get along anyway," I said, a little calmer.

"Max, I really didn't mean to make things worse for you in there! I'm sorry," Lily said, looking awkwardly at her feet. She hated admitting she was wrong. "Let's just go get some coffee or something. We can work on our homework."

I nodded. We weren't back to normal yet, but we would get there. We only had to walk a couple of blocks to get to CeCe's Coffee, but it was cold out. Lily was quiet and I felt like I had to explain why I didn't want to pull another prank right now.

"I just want to lie low for a bit," I said as we walked down the street toward downtown. "Emily and Jackson didn't keep their mouths shut and now everyone at school knows I was responsible."

"I heard some of the other androids talking earlier, though, and they think it was pretty cool. You're kind of turning into a rebel." She laughed.

"I'm pretty sure there are more humans throwing me dirty looks and making nasty comments in the halls than androids who think I'm cool," I said, shrugging. "Four different people tried to trip me today."

"They'll get over it," said Lily. "You know how fast people move on. I can wait till things have calmed down again. But we'd better do the next one together."

I nodded, but I was still a little annoyed with her for outing me.

When we got the coffee shop we ordered

our drinks, chose a table by the fireplace, and settled into the cozy armchairs.

"Did I really make things awful for you?" asked Lily. "Humans are always so cruel."

"It wasn't great," I said. I paused, thinking of Oliver and his confusing kindness. "Maybe they aren't all cruel."

Lily stared at me, frowning a little. "Not cruel?" she said incredulously. "Are you serious? After everything they've done?"

"It's just . . ." I stopped. I didn't know how to explain it. Oliver was so different from the other humans I'd known. "There's this guy, Oliver, in detention. He's been . . . nice to me. Defending me in front of the other humans and stuff."

"And you trust him?" Lily said, raising an eyebrow at me. I knew she thought I was being stupid.

"I don't know!" I said, frustrated. "I know I shouldn't. I know he might turn around and stab me in the back. But so far, all he's done is help me and defend me to Emily and Jackson. Even when they turned on him too."

"Don't let this guy manipulate you. You never know what humans actually want. They'll do anything to help themselves. Trusting humans is always a mistake." Lily shrugged.

I took a sip of my drink, thinking over what she had just said. Lily was saying exactly what I knew I should be thinking. But Oliver had stood up for me when he didn't need to put his neck on the line. He could have taken the easy route, but instead he took a stand.

"You really don't think there's any chance he's on our side?" I asked. "I mean, there were humans campaigning for our rights along with our parents. Just because some of the humans we've met so far aren't exactly welcoming . . ."

Lily snorted. "That's an understatement. I guess I always figured those people cared more about looking kind and forward-thinking to the rest of the world than they did about actually helping us. I thought it was all just politics to them. I don't want anything to do with people who are just using me and other androids as tools to make themselves look better. And I'm not going to change my mind just because some random human is nice to you. If you want to hang out with him, go ahead, but I've got to protect myself. I'm not going to be involved."

"You're probably right. But my parents have told me stories about some of the humans they knew back then. Humans who were willing to break the law for them. It's why they were so excited for me to come to AI High."

I frowned.

"Well I'm perfectly happy not being friends with any humans, thanks. And I don't know why your android friends aren't good enough for you," Lily remarked.

"Of course you guys are good enough for me! You're right, I should be careful with Oliver. I don't want to get burned any more than you do." Even as I said this, I knew I wasn't totally on board with her "no human friends ever" policy. Oliver really did seem different to me. But I didn't say anything else. No matter how many times I went through it, nothing changed. There wasn't some magic thing I'd missed that could prove what Oliver's intentions were. I was going to have to decide whether to trust my gut or my brain.

I looked at Lily. "Are you mad at me for not including you in my pranks?" I said, changing the subject.

She smiled a little. "I was for a bit. You know that."

"Well, are we good? I don't want to lose my best friend over this stuff." I looked at my lap. This kind of conversation always made me feel uncomfortable, but there was so much stuff swirling around my head about how Oliver felt about me and androids in general that I couldn't bear not knowing what Lily was thinking.

"We're good. I was upset because the first one was my idea, and I had to talk you into it. And then you went off on your own and I felt like I wasn't getting any credit. Not that I wanted detention, but still." She shrugged. "I'm kind of over it after hearing how detention has been going. I'm glad you managed to get some attention for how the androids at school are feeling, though."

"Do you think there's a better way to do it?" I asked her. "I can't tell if I've made anyone think or if I've just pissed them off."

"Depends who you're talking about, I think. We both know there are humans who aren't ever going to be okay with androids. But there are others who never thought about any of it. They just keep doing what they've always done and they don't realize that sometimes it hurts us."

"I figured we needed to catch their attention first before we could do anything to actually fix the problems," I said. "Maybe I've done enough to try something else now."

"It's been fun to be a bit of a rebel, though, right?" she said, grinning at me.

I grinned back at that. "I guess."

"What happened to my quiet friend?" she teased. "I thought you'd keep your head down. Maybe try to get your parents to send you to an android school next year. Instead you're thinking about how to get the humans to get along with us."

I laughed sheepishly. "I guess my parents'

protest stories had a bigger effect on me than I thought."

"Well, I hope you don't think yourself to death about Oliver tonight. Either he's genuine or he's not, but there's only one way to find out. Even if I don't think you should bother finding out. Now, we're supposed to be studying." Lily pulled a textbook out of her bag and set it in her lap.

She was right. The only way to figure out what Oliver wanted was to talk to him. And even if he turned out to hate androids as much as most of the other human students, it probably wouldn't change anything. One more human making awful comments or shoving me in the halls wasn't going to make that much of a difference. Tomorrow I'd talk to him.

Even though I'd decided to talk to Oliver, it was harder than I'd thought. Staying out of the humans' way was so normal for me that it took me a while to work up the courage to say hi. We were still repainting in the cafeteria—I'd managed to cover almost the entire wall, and the white paint we were using wasn't thick enough to cover the red letters in a single coat.

I ignored my racing thoughts. I'd already decided that the only way to get answers to my questions was to actually ask them.

"Hey, Oliver," I said casually, taking the spot next to him and grabbing a paint roller. I ignored the glares from Emily and Jackson.

As long as they didn't say anything to me, I planned to ignore them. Dealing with their attitudes was exhausting.

Oliver looked up at me, and I saw surprise on his face before he relaxed and smiled. "Hi," he said. He didn't make a big deal about me talking to him and I was relieved. I was having enough trouble dealing with my own fears and judgments about humans without having to deal with other people's too.

"Did you do anything fun last night?" I asked him, cringing at how awkward I sounded.

"Not really. Too much homework. Did you?" he replied.

"Nope. I just got coffee with my friend, Lily."

"Was she the one who outed you the other day?" he asked, interested.

I felt my shoulders tense up. "Yeah."

"Sorry, is that a sore spot?" said Oliver.

"I wasn't thrilled about everyone finding out," I said, relaxing when he didn't seem mad about cleaning up my messes.

"With those two?" he said, raising an eyebrow and looking at Emily and Jackson. "I definitely get it. I'm sorry they've been so horrible to you. I bet you can't wait to get out of here."

"I'm used to it. It's not like they're the only people who act like that." My mouth twisted in disgust. I hesitated before adding, "I'm sorry they've turned on you too."

He shrugged. "I could have stayed out of it, and they would probably have left me alone. Not that they've ever liked me, but they're not usually so outspoken about it. But you don't deserve it any more than anyone else."

"Even though you're all cleaning up after me?" I asked, surprised.

"Nah. They wouldn't have to be here at all if they could keep themselves out of trouble. There's an easy way out of it. They just like having an excuse to say all the things they're always thinking about androids."

"You are very easy-going," I said. "Any other human here would want to get back at me for what I've done." I tried to play it like a joke, but Oliver knew I kind of meant it.

"I know you don't really trust me yet," he said. "It's fine. I can see how you guys get treated around here. I wouldn't trust me either. But I just want you to know—I don't hate androids, and I don't have any problem with you guys coming to school here either."

His expression was open as he said it. He met my eyes calmly, and it didn't seem like he was trying too hard to prove something to me. I felt myself relax a little more, and I even smiled. "Thanks. That helps. I won't lie to you, though. It will take a lot for me to trust any human fully."

"No worries," said Oliver cheerfully.

We painted quietly next to each other for a few minutes. The silence was friendly, though. Neither Emily nor Jackson tried to talk to us today, but they weren't about to go easy on us. They took every opportunity to bump our elbows and shoulders as we were painting to get us to mess up. Several times they left excess paint on their rollers and then swung them over our heads so that paint dripped on us.

The less we reacted, the more annoyed they got, though, and pretty soon Oliver and I couldn't look at each other without risking bursting into laughter. Nora didn't seem to know how to react to any of this. I don't think she liked that I was being friendly with Oliver, but at least she didn't say anything about it. I could ignore her disapproving looks.

Eventually, Oliver and I started talking again.

"So, if you hadn't had homework, what would you have done last night?" I asked. The question felt random and a little forced, but Oliver didn't seem to care.

"Played my guitar," he said. "I've been playing for a few years. I want to write my own songs someday, but right now I'm still just playing covers."

"Really?" I said. "I play too! Acoustic or electric?"

"I like acoustic better," Oliver said, smiling. "Besides, my parents don't want me to have an amp in the house. They don't like noise."

A shadow crossed his face, but he tried to hide it before I noticed.

"I like both," I said, pretending I hadn't noticed the weird mood shift. I wasn't going to pry.

"Do you want to be a musician, then?" he asked.

I laughed. "Maybe in another life. I'm nowhere near good enough. I want to be a lawyer, I think. At least, I'm planning to go to law school after college. I want to work on android rights cases." I said the last bit quieter. I was pretty sure it might set Emily or Jackson off, and I was enjoying my conversation with Oliver too much. As long as we talked quietly and kept working, the teachers didn't mind.

"You've got to be kidding me," said Oliver. "I'm planning on law school too. Civil rights or family law, I think."

"It's pretty obvious why I would want to do android rights, and I can definitely see why civil rights would be interesting, but why family law?" I asked.

I saw a flash of panic in Oliver's eyes before he got control of his expression again. "It's okay if you don't want to tell me," I said, backtracking. "We hardly know each other. If it's too personal . . ."

Oliver paused. "I just want to help kids when things are going wrong in their families. I thought about going into social work, but it seemed too depressing. I thought it might be interesting in a courtroom, fighting."

His voice had hardened, and I got the feeling there was a lot more to that story. I wondered again why Oliver was in detention. Maybe there was some sort of connection to his family.

"I get it," I said. "I thought about working for a nonprofit or something, but I think I can do more good in court." I paused and a little laugh escaped me. "I can't believe we both want to study law and do something so similar with our lives. I never thought I'd have so much in common with a human."

"I totally understand. You have to protect yourself first. Just try to be open to communication when you meet humans who actually want to learn about you and about androids. I promise we're not all as bad as some of us seem." He smiled faintly. "I know, I know . . . you're thinking about how you're supposed to tell who's genuine and who might actually hate you. I have no answer for that, which is why it makes total sense for you to mostly stay out of our way. I just don't know how it's ever going to get better if humans and androids never talk to each other."

I wanted to thank him for being so understanding, but the words stuck in my throat. I smiled instead. I could feel some of my suspicion with him disappearing. The longer he went on without giving me a reason not to trust him, the easier it was to ignore the voice in my head telling me all humans were awful.

We finished a good chunk of the wall. The first coat was nearly done, and I was glad that I would be out of detention soon if I kept myself out of trouble. Talking to Oliver was starting to give me an idea for how to improve things for the androids at AI High, but I wasn't ready to share it with anyone yet.

As we cleaned up the brushes, Oliver asked, "Do you want to come play guitar with me? I hang out in the band room until the band teacher leaves. We could jam."

I nodded excitedly. "That sounds great! I'll meet you there."

This didn't feel like something he'd do to get close before he turned on me. This felt like being friends.

I drove us over to Oliver's house after the band teacher left for the night, my guitar on the passenger seat. His house was nice, but it didn't seem very homey. There weren't really any pictures on the walls and there was no clutter at all. Like not even dishes by the sink. We went straight up to his room, which was the complete opposite.

Band posters covered his walls, clothes were piled in a corner, and a bookshelf sat next to the unmade bed.

"Aren't your parents home?" I asked.

He shook his head. "Nope." He shrugged, dismissing it. I figured they must be gone a lot. He grabbed a worn guitar from the corner. "Let's play."

I sat on the bed and pulled out my own guitar, strumming a chord to check the tuning. I adjusted my A string a little and then nodded. I hadn't played as much as usual since I started pulling pranks and I missed it.

We played a couple classics first, filling his room with the music and occasionally some mediocre singing. It was amazing. I forgot how much I needed music to help myself relax.

"Do you ever do original stuff?" Oliver asked when we'd been playing for half an hour.

"I want to, but I haven't done much yet," I said. "You want to try to write something together?"

"Yeah," he said, picking a few random notes and then stopping the strings with his palm. "What if we start with a I chord in D major and then go to a IV chord . . ." he trailed off, trying the chords.

I tried them too, testing out ideas for what could come next. As we messed around, recording the bits we liked on our phones and laughing at some of the terrible things we came up with, I couldn't believe how easy it was to get along with him when there wasn't anyone around to judge us. We could be friends without worrying about the problems everyone would have with it.

I could hear Ms. Roberts' annoying voice in my head talking about bringing young humans and androids together. As much as I didn't like her, I had to admit that maybe she had a point.

* * *

The next day, I thought everything was normal. I headed to my android programming class right before lunch, just like always. I liked that class because androids are programmed to understand a lot about computers already, so we cover more advanced stuff than the human programming classes do.

When I got there, I saw Nora talking to Lily. They had their heads together and they looked pretty serious. They weren't talking loudly, but I heard my name and then Oliver's and my heart sank. They shot a look at me and their purple eyes were cold. I tried to get a little closer so I could hear better without them noticing.

"He's betraying us for that human," I heard Nora say. "He's forgotten what team he's supposed to be on."

That was enough for me. I walked to my assigned seat, trying to ignore their stares and whispers.

Their violet eyes pinned me to my seat, and I looked questioningly at Lily. She rolled her eyes and turned to whisper furiously to Nora, who kept glancing over at me.

I knew Lily didn't really like the idea of Oliver and me being friends, but I didn't think she'd really turn on me, I thought. I didn't have a clue what was going on. Everything seemed normal with us in band earlier this morning. I guess Nora couldn't stand the idea either.

I glanced at the clock, hoping I had time to go ask Lily why she was so upset with me, but I was out of time. As class began, I tried to focus. I was so frustrated that I kept forgetting what I was supposed to be doing as my hands hovered above the keyboard. After dealing with the humans being terrible all year the last thing I needed was my friend to turn on me.

Slow down, I thought. *You don't know what she's going to do.* I tried to tell myself that I could have been imagining it, but it felt like there was a huge, dark cloud hanging over Nora and Lily.

When class ended, I tried to catch Lily to talk to her, but she rushed out before I could say anything. I tried to brush it off, but I had a bad feeling in the pit of my stomach.

Soon my suspicions were confirmed. Within an hour, androids I was usually friendly with were refusing to meet my eyes. Some androids I didn't know as well gave me sympathetic smiles, but it seemed like everyone who was friends with Lily or Nora had turned on me.

It was actually worse than the humans' taunts. At least then people acknowledged my existence, even if they didn't like it. And I'd always had my android friends to turn to. I was overwhelmed by the thought of having to make all new friends on top of everything else that was going on.

By the end of the day I was so upset I felt sick. I knew there were other androids at AI High who didn't have a problem with me because not everyone was ignoring me. But my friends were, and that hurt. It was too hard to deal with the humans without friends having your back. The thought of dealing with it all alone made me feel panicked and hopeless. All I'd wanted was for people to treat the other androids and me better, and somehow I'd just made things worse for myself.

When I got to my locker there was a note taped to it. *I thought you were on our side.* That's all it said. *Our side? Do they mean the androids?* I thought. I couldn't come up with any other meaning for it, but I also couldn't figure out why they'd think I wasn't on their side. I felt like all that I'd been doing over the past few weeks was an attempt at trying to raise awareness about the treatment of androids in this school.

At that moment, Oliver walked past, heading for detention. "You coming?" he asked cheerfully.

"Yeah, be right there," I said, crumpling up the note and shoving it into the bottom of my locker. When I turned to follow him I noticed the hostile looks I was getting from the other androids nearby. It was unnerving the way their eyes followed me down the hall.

Oliver was talking, but I wasn't listening. *Wait, this has to be why they're angry*, I realized as I nearly froze midstride.

"I can't talk now," I said abruptly to Oliver, who was in the middle of some story.

He looked at me in surprise, but as usual, he didn't seem too upset. "Uh, okay, I'll see you in there," he said.

His casual response annoyed me. *Doesn't anything bother him? It's not normal*, I thought.

I could feel a hard ball of anger in my chest. This was Oliver's fault. If he had just left me alone none of this would have happened. Even if he'd just joined in with Emily and

Jackson. Then other androids wouldn't hate me. I wouldn't be an outcast from every single person at this stupid school.

I walked into the cafeteria practically vibrating with rage. When Oliver offered me a paint roller, I took it without looking at him and attacked the wall, splattering paint everywhere but not caring.

"Oh my god, I can't believe you did that!" shrieked Emily, looking outraged. "You ruined my shirt!"

I ignored her. Oliver didn't. "I'm sure he didn't mean to," he said, trying to calm her down. "It—"

"Would you both just leave me alone?" I said coldly, still focusing on the section of wall I was painting. "I don't care about your stupid shirt, Emily, and I don't need any pity-help from you, Oliver!" My voice rose until I was nearly shouting. "You humans ruin everything! Just stay away from me!"

Everyone stared at me in shock. Emily's mouth opened and closed like a fish and Oliver looked like I'd hit him.

"I was just trying to help," said Oliver quietly.

"Yeah, well, I don't want it," I said. "I can take care of myself."

"Friends help each other," said Oliver. He was always so good at standing up for himself without losing it, and a tiny part of my brain admired him for it even while I was so angry.

"Maybe I don't want to be friends," I hissed. "You only talk to me because you're too much of a freak for your own kind to like you." The words slipped out before I could stop them and I could hear the venom in my voice. Guilt curled in my stomach at the hurt look on Oliver's face, but I couldn't take it back. He looked at me for a moment, like he was looking for a sign that I didn't mean it. I didn't give him one.

I tried to forget how much fun I'd had jamming on our guitars the other night, ignoring the guilt creeping into my stomach.

I ignored everyone for the rest of detention. I blamed Oliver for this mess, and I figured Nora wouldn't have anything to say to me either. Everything had been fine before she went and told Lily. Given that Lily wouldn't talk to me at all, she must have been pretty upset with me.

That surprised me. I talked to her about Oliver, and while she didn't really understand why I was giving him a chance, I didn't think she was mad at me for it. Well, problem solved, I thought. Oliver and I aren't friends.

The rational part of me that kept whispering that this wasn't Oliver's fault was stubborn. As I calmed down a little, I realized I was angry with Lily too. She'd had no reason to make everyone hate me. I thought she was my best friend. I would never have done something like this to her.

* * *

News spread quickly in this school. By the next morning, androids were meeting my eyes again, smiling at me, saying hi. Clearly my outburst at Oliver was common knowledge, and I guess it was enough for them to forgive me.

Lily met me on my way into school. "So

did you study for the human and android relations test?" she asked like nothing had ever happened.

I paused, taken aback. "Not as much as I should have," I said, trying to act as normal as she was. My emotions were in complete chaos, though. Anger, hurt, confusion, and guilt all swirled around me as I tried to understand what had happened. All I could do was hope Lily didn't notice while I tried to figure it out.

Lily laughed, totally oblivious. "Whatever, Max, you always do great. See you later!" She bounced off down the hallway, clearly in a good mood. I just stared after her, wishing I knew how to feel about this whole situation—and what to do about it.

"Are you coming?" asked Lily.

I closed my locker and followed her out of school. She had waited while I finished detention, working on homework in the library. We were supposed to hang out tonight.

I didn't really feel like it, but I was too worried that saying no would upset her. I didn't want her to think I was betraying her for the humans again.

"Yeah, just a sec," I said, swinging my backpack over my shoulder.

"Coffee again?" she said. "Or do you wanna go for a walk on the trail or something?"

"You pick," I said, shrugging.

"Let's go for a walk," she said. She didn't seem to notice that I wasn't that interested in either option. "I love the trail in the spring, when the birds start singing again. It's not too cold today, either."

I nodded and followed her out of the school. The trail started right behind the building, winding into a patch of forest. It made you feel like you'd left town entirely, and normally I loved it here. Today I was too preoccupied by my confusion about Oliver, humans, and the other androids.

It was the beginning of spring, but the leaves hadn't really started to bud yet. Old, dead leaves from last fall carpeted the trail, soggy under our feet. The air was crisp and fresh, and it still held a slight winter chill. I wished I could enjoy it.

"Did you hear about Josh and Katie?" asked Lily.

"What about them?" I said. I tried to disguise how little I cared about whatever Josh and Katie had done, but I didn't think it worked very well.

"He broke up with Jess and now he and Katie are together," she said.

I grunted, giving up on trying to sound interested. Lily frowned at me.

"What is with you? You're not still upset about that stupid human, are you? I was so glad to see you let that go."

I almost told her that, yes, I was still upset about everything that happened with Oliver, but I couldn't stand the thought that she might ditch me again. Instead I just grunted, "Sorry, I'm just tired. Can we not talk for a bit? I just want some fresh air."

She shrugged but let me be, and we walked in silence, taking the fork in the path that took us back to the school.

"I'll see you tomorrow," I said, heading home. I could feel her watching me as I walked away, but I didn't care enough to say anything else.

* * *

When I arrived at detention the next day, it was like nothing had happened. Emily and

Jackson still hated me, Nora said hi like she hadn't turned half the android population against me, and Oliver nodded at me.

Wait, why is Oliver still being nice to me? After what I said to him? I couldn't believe it. It was almost annoying how he could let anything go. But my annoyance was washed away by the wave of relief that swept over me when he showed no sign of being angry.

I took up my usual painting spot and accepted the roller from Oliver.

"Hey," he said. "Did you have a good day?"

"Yeah, I guess," I said cautiously. *Why am I so happy that he's talking to me?* I wondered. I wouldn't be talking to him if he'd gone off on me like that.

"Did you hear about the open mic night at CeCe's Coffee on Saturday?" he asked.

"No," I said. "I haven't been there in a while."

"I was thinking of playing. You could play with me if you want," he said. For the first time he looked a little nervous, his eyes darting back to the wall instead of meeting my own.

"You want me to play with you?" I asked, disbelieving. "Really?"

"Yeah," he said. "We sounded good together, and I thought it might be fun. Besides, I'm kind of nervous about playing alone. I'd rather do it with someone."

I stared at him. He was right, it did sound fun. Jamming with him had been the most fun I'd had since starting school at AI High. I opened my mouth to say that I'd love to, but the words wouldn't come. I just couldn't understand why he didn't seem at all mad at me. I hadn't even apologized.

"Why are you even talking to me?" the words burst out of me. They weren't a challenge, just a genuine question. I was so confused.

"Why shouldn't I talk to you?" asked Oliver. Now he looked just as confused as I felt.

"Um, maybe because I was a total jerk to you?" I said. I knew I sounded rude, but I just couldn't understand why he was acting like nothing had happened.

Oliver shrugged. "I just don't like being mad at people. It's exhausting. I'd rather just let things go. I know you were super stressed. We all say things we shouldn't sometimes."

I didn't know what to say to that, so I just nodded. I felt sick with guilt, even though Oliver really didn't seem upset about how I'd acted. Seeing him forgive without even an apology only made it clear how unfair Lily had been to me.

Friends were supposed to have each other's backs. Instead, Lily had turned on me and gotten everyone else to join her. I didn't know if I could ever feel the same about our friendship now. I felt like I'd always be wondering when I'd do something that would set her off again.

Oliver was the only person at AI High who had never said anything mean to me, never ignored me, never shoved me in the hallway. He had no good reason to be nice to me, but he did it anyway because it was the right thing to do. Once again I wondered why he had landed in detention for so long when he seemed like the last person to end up here. Maybe someday I'd be able to ask him.

I needed to find a way to make it up to Oliver. I didn't know what to say to apologize though. "Open mic night sounds great," I said tentatively. I hoped he could hear how sorry I was in my voice. I just couldn't force the apology past my lips yet. I was too embarrassed. Especially because Jackson and Emily were clearly eavesdropping.

Oliver smiled, his eyes lighting up. "You'll come?" he said.

"Yeah, definitely." I glanced at Nora, glad she was all the way at the other end of the wall. I didn't think she'd heard. I wasn't going to let anything she or Lily or the other androids did stop me from going, though. I was determined not to make that mistake twice.

Oliver was about to say something when Emily said loudly, "Are you planning any other stunts that we're going to have to clean up? Because we're finally almost done with this stupid wall, and I don't want to deal with this anymore."

I stared at her, then raised one eyebrow. "You know there's an easy fix for that? One that has nothing to do with me?" She scowled at me. "You could just keep yourself out of trouble, and then it wouldn't matter to you what I get up to."

Oliver snorted behind me but stayed out of it.

"Or you could learn your place and follow the rules," said Jackson. "You're lucky to even be here."

"Well, you don't have anything to worry about," I said, keeping my voice calm. I wouldn't let Jackson push my buttons today. I didn't want any more trouble. I'd had enough of that for a while. "I've got no plans right now."

I was actually looking forward to detention the next day. It was my last one. For a while it had seemed like I would be in detention forever, and I had accepted that. I thought that my pranks were worth it to get people thinking about how the androids were treated. I still thought they were. But after everything that had happened I was ready to try a different way.

I felt light when I walked into the cafeteria for detention. Whatever anyone said today, I wouldn't ever have to see them again. I wouldn't let them bring me down.

"Well, if it isn't the droid and the traitor,"

said Emily when I walked in. Oliver was behind me.

"And a good afternoon to you, too, Emily," I said. I almost pretended to tip my imaginary hat at her, but I decided that was too much.

My response startled her. She'd been expecting me to ignore her or maybe make a snarky comeback.

"Whatever," she said, scowling and crossing her arms over her chest.

"Did someone reprogram you last night?" asked Jackson, coming to stand next to her.

"Ah, if only," I said airily. "If someone wiped you two from my memory, I could use the storage space for things that actually matter to me."

Oliver snorted, unable contain his laughter anymore. "I'm a pretty good hacker for a human. I could try if you want," he said jokingly.

Jackson and Emily seemed totally unsure of how to deal with my new attitude. Nora was looking at me like she'd never seen me before either.

"Seriously?" Nora's purple eyes flashed. "After everything, you're back to hanging out with that human?"

I met her gaze squarely. "Oliver may be human, but at least he didn't turn half the school against me." I felt a pang when I thought of how Lily, my supposed best friend, had turned on me so easily, but I pushed it away. I wasn't going to let that get to me right now.

Her jaw clenched. At that moment Emily turned to her. "You don't get to be mad that he's hanging out with a human. He's lucky a human even bothers to look at him."

Oliver and I looked at each other in disbelief. "Emily, it almost sounds like you support our friendship when you say things like that," Oliver responded dryly.

"Ew, obviously not! But at least he wants to hang out with someone better than he is. The rest of the androids are perfectly happy to keep hanging out with their lowlife android friends."

I felt the anger flare in my belly. *Not letting it get to me*, I reminded myself.

"Lowlife?" exclaimed Nora, outraged. "Androids are worth ten humans each!"

Oliver and I slowly took a step back, moving away from them. "Do you think they know that neither of them can convince the other?" I whispered to him.

Oliver rolled his eyes. "That's people for you. When they get angry enough about something, they do things that don't make any sense."

Suddenly I felt my light-hearted mood evaporate. I looked at Oliver seriously. "I'm really sorry for lashing out at you," I said. "I know you already said you understood, but I still need to apologize. It wasn't cool of me to treat you so badly after you'd only ever been kind to me."

"I meant it when I said it was fine," said Oliver. "This year has not been an easy time for androids. I know it seems like all of the humans don't want you here. But I know there are others who are excited about the integration. We need to do a better job to make you feel welcome, and to change other humans' minds.

They obviously aren't listening to you, so it's up to us to try. It's the least we can do after the way androids have been treated in this country."

"Thank you. I guess it's true that humans aren't all terrible," I said.

"No, just most of them," said Oliver, laughing along with me.

"For now, maybe," I said. "But maybe that can change." He definitely proved there were humans who weren't so bad. "I really don't know how you manage to be so nice."

Oliver smiled, but it was a sad smile.

"What?" I asked. "What did I say?"

"I just—" he stopped and took a deep breath. "Did you ever wonder why I was in here?"

"Yeah, but what does that have to do with being nice?"

"My parents haven't really been around," he said. He wouldn't meet my eyes. "They work a lot and sometimes there isn't anyone around to take me to school or pick me up. The school bus doesn't pick up at my house because I technically live outside the district. I really wanted to come to this school, though, so my parents enrolled me. Sometimes if I miss the city bus or it's late I have to walk, and then I'm late for school. Which means detention." He shrugged. "I don't mind detention, really. I'd have to wait around for the night bus home, anyway."

He looked embarrassed, but I felt bad for him. He was doing everything he could to come to school at AI High and he was ending up in detention for it. "Have you told any of the teachers? Maybe they could help. You could hang out in the library after school instead or something."

"It's okay, I don't want to make trouble. My parents have enough to worry about and they might decide it's not worth it for me to come here. It's not that big a deal."

It kind of seemed like a big deal to me, but if he was okay I wasn't going to mess things up for him.

"If you ever need a ride, just call me. I'll come get you," I said.

"Thanks," he said. He looked relieved.

Even though his situation stank, I felt a

little bit of warmth in my chest at the fact that he'd trusted me enough to tell me about it. And I understood why being there for people mattered so much to him. "That's why you're interested in law, isn't it?"

"Yeah. I want to help kids who don't have great family situations, or who have it even worse than I do. At least I could help settle custody agreements and stuff so that the kid gets the best deal possible."

"Yeah, I can see why you'd want to do that," I said. "For now, do you want to do something to help the kids at this school?"

His eyes brightened a little. "You've got some sort of plan, don't you?"

"Yeah," I said, talking a little faster out of excitement. "Look at what happened when you just talked to me. I've changed my mind about some things. No more pranks. What this school needs is a way to get the humans and androids talking, not arguing."

"But how do we do that?" he said. "Isn't that what this whole school is supposed to be, humans and androids talking?"

"Yeah, but we don't always take the same classes, and when we're in such big groups it's easy just to stick to what you know. You said there are humans who want to talk to the androids, but who are too quiet or shy or whatever to actually do it. I bet there are androids who feel the same. How else did they manage to open this school?"

Oliver was nodding enthusiastically now. "Yeah, that's true. We just need to bring those people together. If we can get more people mixing, others will follow."

"Exactly. So I was thinking you and I could team up to start an Android-Human Alliance. We could meet after school once a week, and people could bring their interests to share. They could bring food or books or video games—whatever they're really interested in. People love to talk about the stuff they love."

"That's a great idea. Once we get the conversation going over common interests, we can spread it out to more serious topics about how the integration is going and how we could improve it."

Both of us were so excited now that we looked a little feverish. But it felt amazing to have a plan that felt like it would actually do something to make life better at AI High.

"Do you want to invite Lily to the first meeting?" asked Oliver. "I know you guys were really close. You know . . . before all this."

I frowned, thinking about it. I missed her, but I wasn't sure I wanted to be her friend right now. I wasn't sure I'd ever be able to trust her again. Still, changing attitudes like hers was kind of the point. I nodded. "Yeah, let's invite her. I don't know if she'll come, but I'm going to give her a chance."

We finished painting the wall just as detention ended. Oliver and I spent the whole time coming up with ideas for our Android-Human Alliance, and when the last bit of MEATHEAD HIGH disappeared under the second coat of white paint, I felt like we were getting a fresh start. I didn't know if this alliance would actually work, but if humans and androids could start to get along like Oliver and I, it was worth a shot.

ABOUT THE AUTHOR

When she isn't traveling, Claire Ainslie lives in Wisconsin with her two cats, Bonnie and Eejit, where she spends too much time planning interesting futures for herself. She enjoys baking (because she enjoys eating), Irish dancing, soccer, and fresh air. If you can't find her, it's because she's lost in a book.